SAM'S CAR

Barbro Lindgren
illustrated by Eva Eriksson

William Morrow and Company
New York   1982

Printed in the United States of America.
5   6   7   8   9   10

Library of Congress Cataloging in Publication Data
Lindgren, Barbro. Sam's car.
Translation of: Max bil.
Summary: Sam and Lisa fight over a car until Mother intervenes.
[1. Sharing—Fiction.]
I. Eriksson, Eva, ill. II. Title.
PZ7.L65852Sac   [E]   82-3437
ISBN 0-688-01263-9   AACR2

SAM'S CAR

Look, here's Sam.

Look, here's Sam's car.

Lisa comes.

Lisa wants to drive the car.

Lisa is not allowed
to drive the car.

Lisa smacks Sam. *Ow.*

Sam smacks Lisa.

Ow. Ow. Lisa hurts.

Tears flow.

Mommy brings another car.

Sam is happy.
Lisa is happy.

Toot, says Lisa's car.
Toot, toot says Sam's car.

other books about Sam

SAM'S COOKIE

SAM'S TEDDY BEAR